DEDICATION

To Mom and Dad. Thank you for instilling

in me a love of all animals. I'm still sorry

I cut off our cat's whiskers

when I was seven.

Gobble Gobble Mr. Wobble

authorbcummings@gmail.com

ISBN: 978-1-951597-02-3 (paperback)
ISBN: 978-1-951597-01-6 (ebook)

Library of Congress Control Number: 2019914999

Illustrations by Zuzana Svobodová
Book design by Zuzana Svobodová, Maškrtáreň
Editing by Laura Boffa

First printing edition 2019.

Boundless Movement

Visit www.authorbcummings.com

GOBBLE GOBBLE MR. WOBBLE

BECKY CUMMINGS   ZUZANA SVOBODOVÁ

Word traveled quickly on the farm
that the grand Thanksgiving Day
feast was Thursday, just a few days
away. Farmer Joe came to the barn
to share the news with Wobble the
turkey.

"This year, we'll be having you for
dinner. It's time you got ready,"
Farmer Joe said with a smile.

Wobble couldn't believe it! His eyes popped open. He shook all over. "I'm the dinner guest!" he exclaimed with joy. He sprang into a happy dance, flapping his feathers and creating quite the dust storm. This would be his first Thanksgiving Day feast. He wanted to be ready. He started to prepare himself!

On Sunday, he fancied his feathers and plucked out the old ones. Then, he fluffed his gobbler. Next, he used a little turkey drool to spike his hair. Wobble admired himself in the mirror.

MARVELOUSO!

On Monday, Farmer Linda came to feed Wobble extra food. "There you go, baby. You eat up and get big and strong," she said with joy.

Wobble couldn't believe his luck. "Extra food this week, too. Score!" he whooped. He made sure to eat carefully so his feathers stayed neat. He did not want to be sticky or dirty on the big day.

GOBBLE LEI HE HO

On Tuesday,
Wobble worked
on his perfect gobble to greet the farmer
and his human guests. First, he sang a few warm-up
songs about some farmer called Old MacDonald. Next,
he let out the loudest gobble. That startled the cows to
moo. Which made the ducks quack. The barn got loud!

On Wednesday, Wobble planned to go to sleep nice and early. He was ready to celebrate a day of GIVING and LOVE! Wobble finished reading his book about good table manners. Then, he said a little prayer.

"I'm so thankful to be the dinner guest.
I love Thanksgiving!"

Thursday was Thanksgiving. The barn mouse kept trying to make Wobble take a walk outside, but he would not go. He could not be late for dinner.

Finally, the farmer came to the barn with his ax in hand. "Time for dinner, my friend. Let's go!" exclaimed Farmer Joe.

They went straight to the wood pile and the farmer chopped some pieces of wood for the fire. "These will do. Now come inside."

Farmer Joe threw the wood in the fire. The house lit up with warmth as the smell of freshly baked apple pie filled the room. Then Farmer Linda opened the oven and steam from the most delicious saucy lasagna poured out. The smells were almost too much for Wobble! He shook with happiness.

The family gathered quickly at the table and the farmer pulled out a chair for his beloved turkey. "Time for a family feast, my friend," said Farmer Joe. "Mr. Wobble would you like to say, I mean gobble a few words?" Wobble let it all fly out. "Gobble lei he ho, Gobble lou too who, Gobble tee, Gobble dee, Gobble daa!

I am thankful for your love towards me
and my beautiful barn where I live.
But today, most of all,
I am thankful for
lasagna!"

Do you love animals? I do too. That's why I became a vegetarian a few years ago. That means I don't eat them anymore. You can try it too by encouraging your family to pick a day of the week to go meatless! This means each meal or snack has no meat. You might be surprised at all the yummy choices, plus your heart will be happy knowing you made a difference in an animal's life!

Fuel Up
With Fruit!

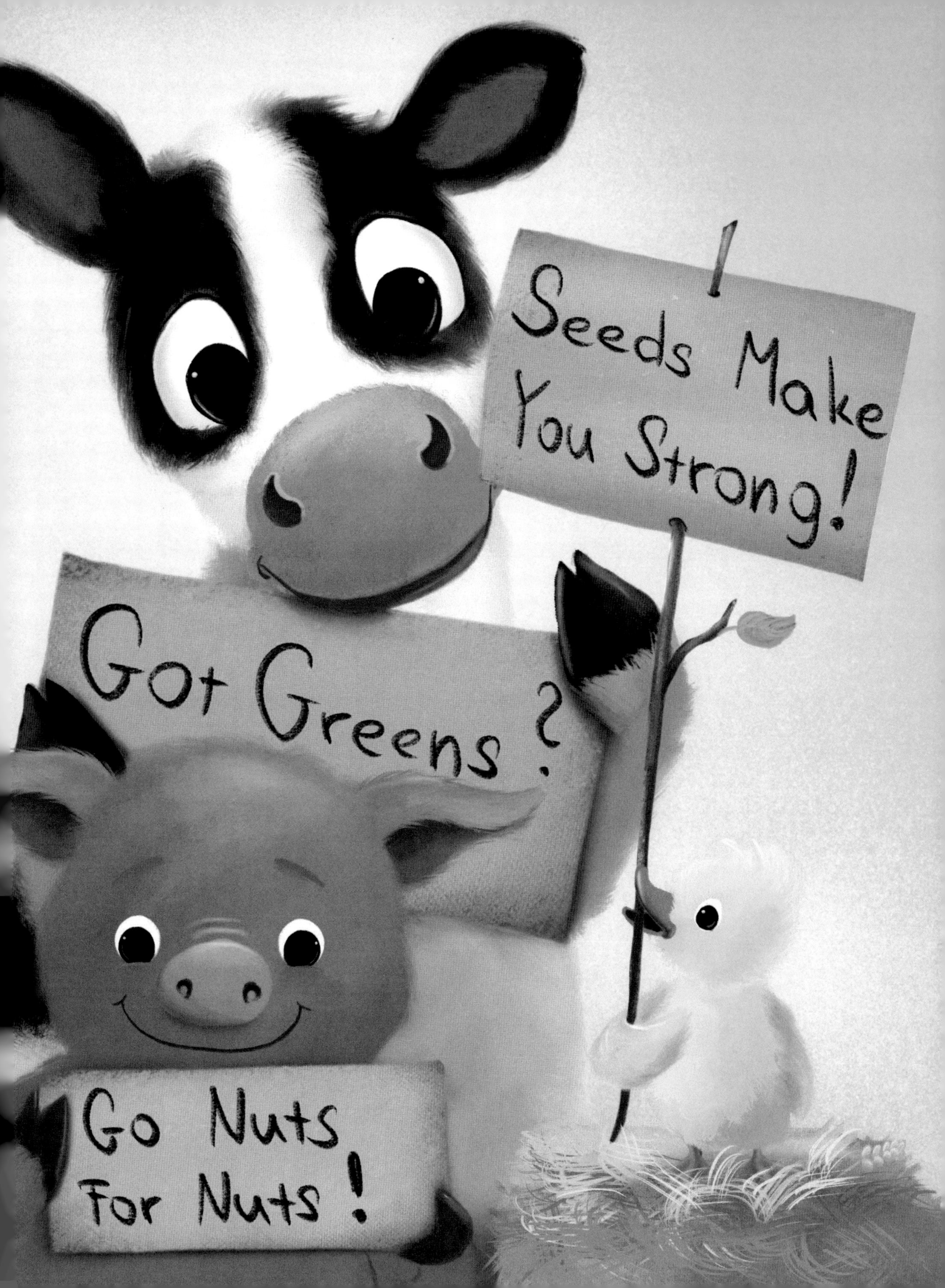
Seeds Make You Strong!
Got Greens?
Go Nuts For Nuts!

LASAGNA

Main Ingredients

1 package lasagna noodles
1 package vegan mozzarella
2 jars favorite tomato sauce (or homemade)
1 1/2 packages firm tofu
1 package vegan hot Italian sausage
1/4 cup nutritional yeast
2 cloves fresh garlic
1 tbsp Italian seasoning
1/4 cup any unflavored, unsweetened plant milk
salt & pepper to taste

1. Prepare the noodles according to the package.

2. Prepare the vegan sausage according to the package until it is fully cooked and broken into crumbles. Add the sauce and set aside.

3. In a food processor add the tofu, salt, pepper, garlic, nutritional yeast, Italian seasoning and plant milk. Puree until mostly smooth with some texture left.

4. In a large baking pan, add a thin layer of sauce, then noodles, then the tofu mixture, more sauce, and then mozzarella cheese. Repeat this pattern until all the noodles are used up.

5. Cover it in tin foil and bake at 350 degrees for an hour. Uncover and bake for another 10 minutes. Allow it to cool for 10 minutes before slicing.

VEGGIE TURKEY PLATTER

Main Ingredients

Roasted red pepper hummus
Rainbow carrots
Peppers

For the Hummus

1 can drained chickpeas
2 tbsp tahini
1/2 squeezed lemon
1 tsp cumin
1 tsp ground coriander seeds
1/4 cup roasted red peppers (can be from a jar)
2 tbsp olive oil (more if needed)
1 clove fresh garlic
salt & pepper to taste

1. Put all of the ingredients in a blender and puree until smooth.

2. Arrange your veggies to look like a turkey. Place the dip in a bowl or use half an empty pepper as a bowl.

These recipes are courtesy of vegan chef Heather Partridge. She loves cooking healthy, plant-based meals. Finding ways to take classic family favorites and veganize them is her passion! For more meal ideas, visit Heather's Instagram page CT_planteater!

Dear Readers,

Thank you for reading *Gobble Gobble Mr. Wobble* to your child or children.
I hope it makes you laugh and think about all you are thankful for in your lives.

If you feel *Gobble Gobble Mr. Wobble* should be shared with others, the best way to help it reach more children is to leave an honest review on Amazon and share it on social media. Tag me with @authorbcummings. Your words and photos will help others learn about my book and encourage me to keep on writing.

If you enjoyed this book, be sure to check out my other books such as *My Magical Words*, *My Magical Choices*, *My Magical Dreams*, and *The Magic of Me: A Kid's Spiritual Guide for Health and Happiness*.

Your support is a blessing. Thank you!

With love,

Becky

Becky Cummings is an author, teacher and mom of three. She loves kids and speaking her truth. Becky is blessed to combine these passions by writing children's books that spread messages of love, hope, faith, health, and happiness. When she isn't writing, you might find her salsa dancing, eating a veggie burrito at her favorite Mexican joint, or traveling to new places! Becky is available for author visits and wants to connect with you so be sure to visit her on Facebook fb.me/authorbcummings, or Instagram and visit her website, www.authorbcummings.com.

Zuzana Svobodová is an illustrator. She uses both digital and traditional techniques, as well as the world of fantasy delivered happily by her two children to bring stories to life. When she isn't working on illustrations, she enjoys drawing, doing and teaching yoga, dreaming and baking sweets.

Made in the USA
Las Vegas, NV
21 November 2020